Also illustrated by Anastasiya Archipova:

Favourite Grimm's Tales
Favourite Tales from Hans Christian Andersen
Hansel and Gretel

Translated by Polly Lawson

First published in German under the title *Schneeweisschen und Rosenrot* by Esslinger Verlag
J.F. Schreiber 2010
First published in English by Floris Books 2010
15 Harrison Gardens, Edinburgh, EH11 1SH
www.florisbooks.co.uk

British Library CIP Data available
ISBN 978–086315–726–4
Printed in Belgium.

Jacob and Wilhelm Grimm

Snow White and Rose Red

Illustrated by
Anastasiya Archipova

Floris Books

There was once a poor widow who lived in a little cottage by the woods. In front of the cottage was a garden with two beautiful rose bushes. One had white roses and the other had red roses.

The widow had two children who were just like the roses. One was called Snow White and the other Rose Red. They were as good, hard-working and cheerful as any two children in the world. Snow White was quieter and more gentle than Rose Red, who loved to run about in the meadows and fields, looking for flowers and catching butterflies. Snow White would sit at home with her mother, helping with the housework or reading aloud to her when there was no work to be done.

The two children loved each other so much that they went hand in hand whenever they left the cottage.

Snow White would say, "We will never leave each other."

Rose Red would answer, "Not as long as we live."

And their mother would add, "Whatever one has, she should share with the other."

Often they would walk in the woods, hand in hand, gathering red berries. No animal ever harmed them, but came up to them without fear. The little hare would eat a cabbage leaf out of their hands; the roe deer grazed beside them and the hart bounded joyfully past them, while the birds stayed on their branches singing their merry songs.

No accident ever befell Snow White and Rose Red. If they stayed late in the woods and night fell, they would lie side by side on the moss and sleep until morning, and their mother would know they were safe.

One night in the wood, they saw a lovely child in a shining white dress sitting near where they lay. The child stood up and smiled at them, but said nothing and walked away. When they looked around they saw that they had been sleeping on a clifftop and, if they had walked a few steps further in the darkness, they would have fallen over the edge. Their mother told them that they had met the angel who watches over good children.

Snow White and Rose Red kept their mother's cottage very clean and tidy. In summer Rose Red brought her mother a bunch of flowers every morning, with a rose from each bush. She put them beside her bed before she woke up. In winter Snow White lit the fire and hung the kettle on the hook. The kettle was made of brass, but it shone like gold because it had been so well polished.

In the evenings, when the snow was falling, their mother would say, "Snow White, go and bolt the door." Then she would read aloud to them by the hearth, while the two girls sat and span. Beside them a lamb lay on the floor, and behind them on a perch sat a little white dove.

One evening, as they were sitting cosily together, someone knocked at the door. "Quick, Rose Red, go and open the door," said their mother. "It must be a traveller seeking shelter."

Rose Red drew back the bolt, thinking it would be some poor, weary man, but it was not; a bear thrust his thick black head in through the doorway.

Rose Red cried out and sprang back, the lamb bleated, the little dove fluttered up into the air and Snow White hid behind her mother's bed.

The bear, however, started to speak: "Do not be afraid, I will do you no harm. I am half frozen and I only wish to warm myself a little in your house."

As soon as the grey dawn came, the two children let the bear out and he trundled off over the snow into the woods.

From then on, the bear came back every evening at the same time. He lay down by the hearth and let the children play with him as much as they wished. They were now so used to him coming that they did not bolt the door until their black companion had come in.

When spring came and the outside world was green once more, the bear said to Snow White, "Now I must go away and I cannot come back all summer."

"Where are you going, dear bear?" asked Snow White.

"I must go into the wood and guard my treasures from the wicked dwarfs. In winter when the ground is frozen hard they have to remain below and cannot work their way up and out, but now that the sun has thawed the earth, they will break through. Then they will search and steal. Whatever they take down into their hollows cannot easily be brought back into the daylight."

Snow White was sad to say goodbye to her friend. When she drew back the bolt of the door and the bear pushed his way out, his fur caught on the latch and a piece of his hide was torn off. Snow White thought she saw a glimpse of gold shining through from underneath, but she couldn't be sure. The bear hurried away and soon disappeared among the trees.

"You poor bear," said their mother. "Lie down by the fire, but be careful not to singe your fur."

Then she called, "Snow White, Rose Red, come out. The bear will not hurt you; he can be trusted." They both came forward, and very cautiously the lamb and the dove came nearer until they were no longer afraid.

"Children," said the bear, "beat the snow a little out of my fur." They fetched a broom and swept the fur clean while he stretched out by the fire and, much at ease, growled contentedly.

Soon the girls got to know and trust their clumsy guest, and began to play mischievous games with him. They tugged at his fur with their hands, put their feet on his back and rocked him back and forth; they took a hazel branch and beat him, and when he growled they laughed. The bear did not mind at all, but when they were too rough, he cried:

"Leave me alive, children,
Snow White, Rose Red,
You'll strike your suitor dead."

When it was time to go to sleep and the others had gone to bed, their mother said to the bear, "In God's name you may stay and lie by the hearth and you will be sheltered from the cold and bad weather."

After a while, their mother sent the children into the wood to gather firewood. They found a large tree that lay felled on the ground, and by the trunk something was jumping up and down in the grass, but they couldn't make out what it was.

When they went nearer, they saw it was a dwarf with a wrinkled old face and a very long snow-white beard. The end of the beard was caught tight in a cleft of the tree, and the little man was jumping like a dog on a leash, not knowing what to do. He stared at the girls with his fiery red eyes and screamed, "What are you standing there for? Can't you come and help me?"

"What has happened to you, little man?" asked Rose Red.

"Silly nosy goose!" answered the dwarf. "I wanted to split the tree to make small logs for the kitchen fire. Thick logs burn the little food that we eat; we don't guzzle as much as you greedy folk. I had already hammered in the wedge and everything was going well, but the cursed wooden wedge flew out and the tree trunk snapped so quickly that I got my lovely white beard stuck in the tree and now I can't get away. And you silly, smooth milk-faces are laughing. Bah, how repulsive you are!"

The children tried hard, but they could not pull the beard out; it was jammed in tight.

"I'll go and get some people to help," said Rose Red.

"You mutton-headed chumps!" screeched the dwarf. "What do you want to fetch more people for? You're two too many already. Can't you think of anything better?"

"Don't be impatient," said Snow White. "I'll soon get you out." She took her scissors out of her pocket and cut off the end of his beard.

As soon as the dwarf was freed, he seized a sack of gold that was hidden behind the roots of the tree and muttered to himself, "Uncivilized rabble, cutting off a piece of my good beard — a pox on you!"

Then he slung the sack on his back, and off he went without even looking back at the children.

Some time later, Snow White and Rose Red went to the stream to catch some fish for supper. As they came to the banks of the stream, they saw something that looked like a big grasshopper hopping towards the water's edge as if it were about to jump in. They ran up, and saw it was the dwarf.

"Where are you going?" asked Rose Red. "Surely you don't want to jump in the water?"

"I'm not a fool!" cried the dwarf. "Can't you see that the cursed fish is trying to pull me in?"

The little man had been sitting there fishing when a gust of wind had blown his beard into his fishing line and it had got tangled. When a big fish had taken a bite on his hook, the weak dwarf couldn't pull it out of the water. As the fish struggled to free itself, it pulled the dwarf after it, and although he tried to clutch at stalks and rushes to steady himself, he would soon be dragged in.

The girls had come along in the nick of time. They held the dwarf tight and tried to free his beard from the line, but beard and line were hopelessly entwined. There was nothing for it but to take out the scissors and cut off the beard — and a little bit was lost.

When the dwarf saw, he screamed, "Do you think that's civil, you toads, to ruin a person's face? Wasn't it enough to spoil the end of my beard, without cutting off the best part of it? I won't be able to show myself to my own people. Buzz off and run till your feet fall off!"

Then he fetched a sack of pearls, which was lying in the reeds and, without saying another word, he hauled it away and disappeared behind a stone.

Soon afterwards, their mother sent the two girls off to town to buy thread, needles, tape and ribbons. As they walked over the heath towards town, they saw a great bird hovering in the air and slowly circling above them. It sank lower and lower until it finally plunged down by one of the many rocks that lay strewn over the heath.

Immediately afterwards the girls heard a piercing cry of pain. They ran towards the sound and saw, to their horror, that the eagle had seized hold of their old friend the dwarf and was about to carry him off.

The kind children held tightly on to the little man and struggled with the eagle until he let go of his prey.

When the dwarf had recovered from his fright, he cried in his screeching voice, "Couldn't you have treated me a bit more carefully? My thin coat is torn into shreds and holes, you awkward, clumsy clots!"

Then he grabbed a sack of jewels and crept under the rocks into his hole.

The girls were already used to his ungrateful ways, and continued on their way to town.

When the girls came back from town over to the heath towards home, they saw the dwarf once again, and took him by surprise. He was emptying his sack of jewels, for he did not think anyone would be passing by so late.

The evening sun shone on the sparkling jewels, and they glittered and gleamed so gloriously that the children stopped to look at them.

"What are you standing there staring for?" screamed the dwarf, as his ashen grey face turned scarlet with rage. He carried on shouting until they all heard a loud growling sound and a black bear came out of the wood.

The dwarf jumped up in fright, but the bear was blocking the entrance to his hidey-hole so he could not escape.

"Dear bear, spare me!" he cried out in terror. "I will give you all my treasures. See my beautiful jewels lying there? Grant me my life. I'm such a scraggy little creature, you would hardly feel me between your teeth. Look, take these two godless girls. They would be tender morsels for you; they're as juicy as young quails. Eat them up for heaven's sake!"

The bear took no notice of his words. He gave the evil creature one single blow with his paw, and he never moved again.

The girls had run away, but the bear called after them, "Snow White and Rose Red, do not be afraid. Wait, I will come along with you."

When they heard his voice, the girls recognized their good friend, and they waited. When the bear was beside them his bearskin fell from him, and there he stood as a handsome young man, dressed all in gold.

"I am the king's son," he said. "I was bewitched by the evil dwarf who had stolen my treasure and condemned me to roam the woods as a wild bear until I should be released by death. He has got what he deserved."

In time, Snow White was married to the prince and Rose Red to his brother, and they shared the great treasures that the dwarf had gathered in his hollow.

Their mother lived for many years peacefully and happily with her children. She took the two rose bushes with her, and they stood in front of her window. Every year they bore the loveliest roses, white and red.